INDIANA JONES
and the
LAST CRUSADE

Storybook Written by Anne Digby
Based on a Screenplay by Jeffrey Boam
Story by George Lucas and Menno Meyjes
Directed by Steven Spielberg

SCHOLASTIC INC.
New York Toronto London Auckland Sydney

ISBN 0-590-42874-8

TM and copyright © 1989 by Lucasfilm Ltd. (LFL). All rights reserved. Published by Scholastic Inc., authorized user.

12 11 10 9 8 7 6 5 4 3 2 1   9/8 0 1 2 3 4/9

Printed in the U.S.A.   34

First Scholastic printing, October 1989

INDIANA JONES
and the
LAST CRUSADE

THE MAN IN THE BROWN HAT

Only once did somebody get the better of Indiana Jones. Indy was twelve years old at the time and still learning. It was in the battle for the priceless, jewel-encrusted treasure known as the Cross of Coronado.

The man who beat him wore a brown fedora hat. Indy never saw him again, but he wears the man's hat to this day.

It was on the same occasion that Indy learnt how useful a whip could be.

One morning in 1912 the young Indiana Jones rode out with his Boy Scout troop to a local cave inside towering cliffs. The Scoutmaster had told them all to keep together but when they reached the cave Indy wanted to explore. He and another Scout, Herman, slipped away from the rest of the troop and rode through cool, dark passageways into the secret heart of the cave.

Travelling down through a tunnel full of snakes and spiders, they reached an underground chamber. Then they stopped dead in their tracks.

A gang was looting buried treasure in there!

The leader was a cool, tough-looking man who wore a battered brown fedora hat. He was turning a jewel-encrusted cross over and over in his hands. The cross sparkled brightly and the blue eyes under the hat's brim sparkled back.

"It's the Cross of Coronado!" whispered Indiana in amazement. "Cortes gave it to him in 1520! It proves that Cortes sent Coronado in search of the Seven Cities of Gold."

"How do you *know* all this stuff, Indy?" mouthed Herman in awe. He'd noticed long ago that Indiana Jones was a walking encyclopaedia.

Indy's mother was dead. His father was Professor Henry Jones, the famous medieval scholar and Indy had been reared since babyhood on a rich diet of knowledge. By the age of five he knew the Greek, Arabic, Hebrew and Sanskrit alphabets better than

his own. Named Henry, after his father, he had adopted instead the name of their dog — Indiana. He liked it better.

"I just do," whispered Indiana impatiently. "That cross is an important artefact. It belongs in a museum. You run back and find the others: have them bring the sheriff!"

"What are you going to do?"

"I'll think of something . . . get going!"

As soon as the cross had been laid down and the men's backs were turned, Indiana snatched it and ran.

With the gang in hot pursuit there followed a chase of unbelievable thrills, a foretaste of his adult adventures to come.

The greatest excitement took place on board a moving circus train. All the circus animals and sideshows were housed inside special railway freight carriages. Indy had leapt aboard the moving train to escape the gang but they were right behind him.

Hanging grimly on to the Cross of Coronado as he worked his way along the train, Indy didn't have just the gang to contend with. He narrowly escaped a car-full of squirming snakes, a crocodile's jaws, a Bengal tiger, and a fierce black rhino.

However, it was the confrontation with the fierce African lion that was the most terrifying episode of all. He had dropped the cross right by the lion's feet! That was the moment that Indiana Jones discovered the singular usefulness of whips.

On this occasion it was the lion tamer's. Indy grabbed it from the hook. Inwardly quaking, he cracked it in the lion's direction. Once. Twice. On the third crack, the angry animal backed away and Indy was able to dart forward and retrieve the cross.

But he was still trapped in the cage.

A hatch opened overhead. The man in the brown hat looked down at him.

"Give me one end of that whip and I'll get you out of there."

Indy tossed it up to him. Then, holding tight to the other end, Indy found himself being reeled up to the roof and safety.

From that moment onwards he vowed never to be without a whip of his own.

"You've got heart, kid," said the man, "but that cross belongs to me."

"It belongs to Coronado!" said Indy, racing away with it. After one last exciting chase, he leapt to safety from the train as it reached town.

Watched with sneaking admiration by the man in the brown hat, Indiana ran along the rail tracks as fast as he could go, clutching the precious cross, until he reached the street where he lived.

He burst into his father's study, panting for breath.

"Dad!"

"Out!" said his father. The professor's study was a no-go area. Right now he was sitting at his desk. His head was bent over a faded volume, its pages made of ancient parchment. There was a beautifully illuminated picture of a stained-glass window on the open page. The professor was slowly and laboriously copying some details from it into a thick notebook. He always referred to this notebook as his Grail Diary.

"This really is important, dad!"

"Then wait — count to twenty," replied his father, still deeply immersed. "*Junior!*"

Professor Henry Jones in this mood was not to be crossed. Very quietly, Indiana began to count. As he did so his father muttered, without looking up:

"This is also important . . . and it can't be hurried. It's taken nine hundred years to find its way from a forgotten box of parchment in the sepulchre of St. Sophia in Constantinople to the desk of the one man left in the world who might make sense of it."

"Dad!" began Indy, as soon as he'd got to twenty. "Look." He started to pull the cross out from inside his shirt. "I was in the cave with the Scout troop and . . ."

"Now in Greek," commanded the Professor.

In an agony of frustration, the boy began to count in Greek. His father was just finishing his sketch and murmuring to himself:

"May he who illuminated this, illuminate me."

Suddenly, hearing voices outside, Indy slipped out of his father's study and closed the door behind him. Herman was bursting into the house, followed by the sheriff.

"I brought him, Indy! I brought the sheriff!"

Indiana ran up to the sheriff.

"Sheriff!" he said, choking with relief. "They almost got me, but . . ."

"All right, son — do you still have it?"

"Yes sir — right here!" said Indy proudly, handing over the Cross of Coronado.

The sheriff took it casually.

"I'm glad to hear that because the rightful owner of this cross says he won't press charges if you give it back. On account of your being a minor he won't press charges . . ."

"PRESS CHARGES?" asked Indy, aghast. "WHAT FOR?"

Even as he spoke, a tall figure walked in through the front door, politely removed his brown fedora hat and smiled sardonically. Outside in the street, Indy glimpsed some of his men.

"Charges for theft, of course," said the sheriff.

As Indy began to protest, he snapped: "No far-fetched stories, son. This gentleman's got witnesses, five or six of them."

The sheriff then solemnly handed over the cross to the man with the brown fedora and they exchanged knowing looks. Indy knew it was hopeless. He'd been completely outwitted.

The sheriff left. But the man turned to Indy and gave him a look of respect.

"You lost today, kid, but that doesn't mean you have to like it."

He held up his hat by the crown and slowly, almost as though he were performing an initiation ceremony, he placed it on Indiana's head.

"Here."

Indiana drew himself up to his full height and gazed up into the man's face. Blue eyes met blue eyes.

"The Cross of Coronado is four hundred years old and it still has a long way to go," said Indy. "I aim to be around."

The man walked straight out and handed the artefact to somebody sitting in a car, waiting for it, someone with an evil face, wearing a white panama hat, who reached out a hand and took the cross and then handed the gang leader a thick wad of banknotes.

So he was just doing a job! thought Indy. Very efficient. And that pasty-faced slob in the panama hat is the "rightful owner of the cross", so-called. Well, we'll see.

Indiana Jones had no intention of ever forgetting that pasty face. He'd get back at him one day.

He fingered the crown of the fedora, sitting it more comfortably on his head. He liked the feel of it. Its owner was tough, a fighter. And in the middle of the battle on the moving train, he'd pulled Indy clear of the circus lion! Saved his life — he hadn't needed to do that.

Indy pulled the brim of the hat down over his eyes. It was amazing how well it fitted. It could have been made for him.

★★★   ★★★

Indiana Jones the man met up with the thief in the white panama hat twenty-four years later. They were on a storm-battered Spanish cargo boat in the middle of the ocean.

Dodging sailors' knives and flying fuel drums, Indy wrested away the Cross of Coronado and jumped off the ship only seconds before it blew up.

He grabbed a lifebelt, held on to his brown fedora hat and watched the fragments of a white panama go floating by amongst the wreckage of the shattered ship.

Indy was on his way home. The cross would rightfully end up in a museum at long last — the museum of the American University where Indiana Jones, PhD, was now Professor of Archaeology.

INTERVIEW FOR A JOB

Dr. Indiana Jones, in horn-rimmed spectacles and professorial tweeds, addressed the packed college lecture hall in New York.

"The Lost Continent of Atlantis! King Arthur's Knights of the Round Table! Nothing more than charming romantic nonsense. Archaeology is our search for *fact*."

His students hung on to every word. They'd waited long enough. After his adventure on the high seas Indy was two weeks late back at the university.

"Next week — Egyptology, beginning with the excavation of Naukratis by Flinders Petrie in 1885. Miss Appleton has this term's reading list for you."

After the lecture, Indy couldn't wait to grab Professor Brody. Marcus Brody was an Englishman and a lifelong friend of his father's. He was also Director of the University Museum. He had large funds at his disposal and would never rest until his museum excelled even the Ashmolean in Oxford, where as a young undergraduate Marcus had whiled away many happy hours amongst the antiquities.

"Marcus, I've got it! Something you've wanted for years and I've wanted all my life."

From the pocket of his tweed jacket he produced the Cross of Coronado.

"That's it!" gasped Marcus.

"For you, Marcus. For the museum."

The elderly Englishman handled it reverently.

"This will find a place of honour among our Spanish acquisitions. And your fee, Indy?"

"We'll discuss it later, Marcus. Over champagne."

Fortune and glory.

Humming happily to himself, Indy gave a crowd of students the slip and went through to his inner office. All his mail was waiting for him, including a thick package with a Venice postmark. He crammed it into his pockets intending to look at it later. Right now he felt like a break; a walk in the fresh air. It was a beautiful day.

He stepped out into the college gardens from his office window and was soon walking the city streets.

A black Packard pulled up beside him and men asked him courteously to get inside. Their clothes bulged with guns.

Indy decided not to argue.

They took him to a luxury apartment block on Fifth Avenue and up to a magnificent penthouse.

Indy admired his surroundings. The apartment's reception hall had a great number of rare artefacts on display.

A door opened. The powerful figure of a grey-haired man in a dinner jacket came through to greet him. In the background, Indy could hear tinkling music and the clink of glasses. His host was obviously in the midst of a cocktail party.

"I trust my men didn't alarm you, Dr. Jones. I do apologise, but I need you urgently. My name is Walter Donovan."

"I know your name," said Indy briefly. "A generous benefactor of our University Museum. I must say some of the pieces in your own private collection here are most impressive."

"I have something even more impressive that I would like you to see."

"Certainly, Mr. Donovan."

A flat stone tablet was unwrapped. It was inscribed with letters and symbols. Indy put on his glasses, his interest quickening. He studied it very carefully. The top part was missing, but . . .

"Early Christian symbols. Gothic characters. Byzantine carvings. Middle twelfth century, I'd say."

"That was our assessment as well, Dr. Jones. Can you please translate the inscription?"

Slowly, haltingly, Indy translated:

". . . *whoever drinks the water that I shall give him will have a spring inside him welling up for eternal life . . . Across the desert and through the mountain to the Canyon of the Crescent Moon, broad enough only for one man. To the Temple of the Sun, holy enough for all men. Where . . .*"

Indy paused, looking startled.

"*Where the cup that holds the blood of our Lord resides for ever.*"

"The Holy Grail, Dr. Jones." Walter Donovan was trembling with excitement. "Clues to the whereabouts of the Holy Grail."

"I've heard that bedtime story before," said Indy.

"Think of it, Dr. Jones! *Eternal life.* The gift of youth to whoever drinks from the Grail. Now that's a bedtime story I'd like to wake up to!"

"An old man's dream, Mr. Donovan."

"*Every* man's dream, Dr. Jones. Including your father's, I believe."

Indy stiffened slightly at the mention of his father.

"Well, yes. Grail lore is his hobby."

"His abiding passion, Dr. Jones. And he is the country's leading Professor of Medieval Literature, based at Princeton University."

"The one the students hope they don't get."

"Give the man his due, Dr. Jones. He's the foremost Grail scholar in the world today!" A fanatical expression crossed Walter Donovan's face. "Hard to resist, isn't it? The Holy Grail's final resting-place described in detail!"

"What good is it? There's no location given. There are plenty of deserts and canyons and mountains in the world — where do you start looking?"

Walter Donovan took an ancient leather-bound volume out of a drawer, handling it gently.

"I have to tell you, Dr. Jones, that an attempt to recover the Grail is currently under way. You will recall that it was lost for a thousand years before being found again by three Knights of the First Crusade. Three brothers."

"Sure," said Indy, glancing at the old volume with interest. "After finding the Grail, only one brother came back. One died on the way. The one who came back imparted his tale to a Franciscan friar."

"*This is the friar's manuscript,*" Donovan snapped out triumphantly. "It tells of two 'markers' the knights left behind that enable us to locate the Grail. The first marker is this incomplete Tablet which you have just translated."

"And the second?" asked Indy.

"Ah yes, the second clue. According to the Franciscan friar's account, it is entombed with the second Knight, the one who died on the way back. Our project leader, who has researched the subject for years, believes that the tomb can be located in the city of Venice, Italy."

"Well now," said Indy. "And what happened to the third brother anyway. I forget. There were three knights, weren't there?"

There was a little tremble in Walter

Donovan's voice as he replied.

"The third brother stayed behind with the Holy Grail. He became — he still is until this day — the Keeper of the Grail. Are you not intrigued, Dr. Jones? Can you not see we're about to complete a great quest that began almost two thousand years ago. We're only one step away."

"Let's hope you don't hit a snag," said Indy casually.

"We have."

"How come?"

"Our project leader has vanished, Dr. Jones. Along with all his research. We have received a cable from his colleague, Dr. Schneider, who has no idea of his where-abouts or what has become of him."

He paused.

"We want you to pick up the trail. Find the man and you find the Grail."

"Very interesting but I think you've got the wrong Jones, Mr. Donovan. Why don't you try my father?"

The reply came after another pause. When it came, Indy felt as though a cold, icy hand were running down his spine.

"We already have. Your father is our project leader. Your father is the man who's disappeared."

THE GRAIL DIARY

Worried, Indiana Jones burst into his father's empty house. Marcus Brody, his Dad's oldest friend, was by his side. They had driven from New York in the Ford at top speed.

"I've watched you and Henry grow apart over the years, Indy. I've never seen you this concerned about him before," said Marcus.

"He's an academic! A bookworm, not a field man!"

Professor Henry Jones' study had been ransacked.

"They've even gone through his mail," said Marcus, staring at a pile of torn envelopes and scattered paper.

"Mail! That's it, Marcus!" shouted Indy. He rummaged through his pockets and found the thick brown packet he'd stuffed there earlier. "Venice, Italy! How could I be so stupid?"

He took one last look at the postmark then ripped open the package. There was a small, thick journal inside.

"What is it?" asked Marcus as Indy flipped through the pages.

There was page after page of handwritten notes and careful little drawings.

"It's Dad's Grail Diary."

"Why did he get it sent to you?" frowned Marcus.

"I don't know. For safe keeping. And a cry for help, maybe." Indy frowned as he looked round at the ransacked study. "*Somebody* wants this Grail Diary pretty badly." He handed it over to Marcus. "It's all there. A lifetime's worth of research and knowledge." He looked his father's best friend in the eye. "Do *you* believe the Grail actually exists?"

"The search for the Holy Grail is the search for the divine in all of us," replied the older man. "If you want *facts* I have none for you, Indy. At my age I'm willing to take a few things on trust. If your father believes the Grail is real, so do I."

Indiana Jones looked thoughtful, then spoke:

"Let's call Walter Donovan. I've decided to take that ticket to Venice after all."

"And I'm coming with you, son," said Marcus Brody.

The next day Donovan saw them into his private biplane and wished them luck. He was placing an apartment in Venice at their disposal. Henry Jones' colleague, Dr. Schneider, would meet them on arrival.

As Indy raised his brown fedora hat in farewell Walter Donovan whispered in his ear:

"Be very careful, Dr. Jones. Don't trust *anybody*."

Indy was to remember those words.

In the plane he relaxed and made a careful study of the Grail Diary. One thing that interested him was a rough sketch of a stained-glass window, with some Roman numerals noted below. He remembered it from childhood — that old book his dad had been looking at.

He also discovered that his father had taken a rubbing of Walter Donovan's Grail Tablet, with the top part missing, of course.

It was on a separate piece of paper, tucked inside the Diary.

The last lap of their journey to Venice was by water bus. As they approached the quay, they could see the militia everywhere. This was the 1930s and Italy, like Hitler's Germany, was in the grip of fascism.

It had been arranged that Dr. Schneider would meet them on the quay. "How will we know him when we see him?" wondered Marcus. "Maybe he's holding a sign," replied Indy.

When they disembarked a lovely young woman came up to them, blond-haired and bright-eyed.

"Dr. Jones?"

"Yes?" Indy was instantly smitten.

"I knew it was you — you have your father's eyes."

She then turned, with a dazzling smile: "Professor Brody?"

"That's right," replied Marcus, puzzled.

"Well, I'm Dr. Schneider. Dr. Elsa Schneider."

Indy's eyebrows shot up in delight and surprise.

As they walked across the piazza he whisked a flower from a street vendor's stall and presented it to her. They exchanged flirtatious glances. "Tomorrow I'll steal you another," promised Indy.

"Look here, I hate to interrupt this," said Marcus. "The reason we are here . . ."

"Yes, I know," said Elsa briskly. "I have something to show you. An interesting scrap of paper."

They had reached an old building — the city library. On the steps outside, Elsa produced the scrap of paper and handed it to Indy.

"Your father was working at a table, in this library here. He sent me off to the map section to fetch some very old plans of the city of Venice. That was the last I saw of him. When I got back to his table, he'd gone. Completely vanished. All his papers had gone, too — except for this one scrap which I found near his chair."

On the slip of paper there were simply three Roman numerals: III, VII and X.

"Three, seven and ten," said Elsa as they entered the old building and walked across its great mosaic floor. "I've been trying to work out what those numbers mean ever since he disappeared."

Indy took in his surroundings at a glance. There were some large stained-glass windows. Four massive marble columns rose up to support the roof. It felt like being in church.

"Yes, we're on holy ground," explained Elsa. "This used to be the chapel of a Franciscan monastery. Excuse me, I just have to go and check something at the reference counter."

As Elsa's heels clicked off across the mosaic floor, Indy grabbed Marcus' arm and pointed to the nearest stained-glass window. It depicted a Knight of the Crusades.

"Marcus, I've seen this window before. Look!" He whipped out the Grail Diary and turned to the page he had noticed on the aeroplane.

"It's the same!" exclaimed Marcus. "And the same Roman numerals written underneath: III, VII and X."

"Dad was on to something here," said Indy, quickly putting the Diary away as he saw that Elsa was coming back. "He sent me this precious volume for a reason. Until we find out why, nobody sees it, okay?"

"Look Elsa," said Marcus, pointing. "This window seems to be the source of the Roman numerals."

"You're right," exclaimed Elsa in excitement.

But Indy was even more excited. He had just noticed the Roman numeral III worked into the top of one of the marble pillars. He pointed.

"Don't you get it? Dad was looking for the Knight's Tomb somewhere *in here*. It's somewhere in the library. You said yourself that it used to be a church. The numerals are a kind of grid reference. There's the first one, *three*. Spread out and find the *seven* and *ten*!"

He ran around, eyes darting everywhere. He found the *seven* next! It was on one of the book shelves, placed centrally between the columns. But where was the *ten*?

Nearby was a ladder leading up to a loft where books were stored. On impulse, Indy climbed it. From the loft he was now able to look down on the elaborate tile patterns of the mosaic floor far below. From this bird's-eye vantage point something leapt to the eye — a tile design in the shape of the letter X!

"X marks the spot!" he cried, slithering down the ladder fast.

He began to prise up the slab right at the centre of the X.

"Look!" he shouted.

Elsa and Marcus gathered round. It was the opening to a secret tunnel. The three of them stared down at the two-foot-square hole. It seemed to descend right into the bowels of the earth.

Cold air and a wet, rancid smell rushed up at them.

"Bingo," said Indy.

"You don't disappoint, Dr. Jones. You're a great deal like your father," said Elsa. "Lower me down, will you?"

Admiring her courage, Indy obliged, carefully lowering her into the hole. "And I'm coming with you!" he shouted down.

But first he turned to Marcus and slipped him the Grail Diary. "Keep an eye on this for me."

Marcus pocketed it and watched Indy follow Elsa down into the hole.

Then, kneeling down, he started to push the slab back into place.

He never even heard a man called Kazim creep up behind him.

Kazim struck Marcus on the back of the head with a sharp blow and knocked him out.

AN OUTING IN THE CATACOMBS

They were in the catacombs. There were skeletons everywhere. The skulls grinned at them from out of the darkness as they felt their way along the murky tunnels. All around them was a foul-smelling dankness. The deeper they went, the earlier the burial chambers became.

"If a Knight from the First Crusade is entombed down here, it'll be a long way down," said Indy.

He took Elsa's hand.

"We're on a crusade, too, aren't we?" she said.

"I guess we are," said Indy, with distinctly romantic feelings welling up.

But all around him there was something else welling up! Green slimy water with oil bubbling up to the surface! They had to wade through slicks of the stuff.

"Look at this," said Elsa, peering at markings on the wall. "We're in a tenth-century burial chamber."

"We must be getting there."

They were, except that now the water was knee deep, the passageway narrow and . . .

"Rats!" screamed Elsa. There were hundreds of them.

Indy pulled her up on to a narrow ledge, just clear of the water, and they edged their way along it, the rats swirling beneath their feet. They rounded a corner. There in front of them was the final burial chamber.

Here the rank water was much deeper; but on a stone plinth that jutted up in the middle of the chamber were some brass-bound coffins. Surely here they would find what they were looking for!

To get at them they had to wade almost chest deep through the water which was now black and putrid. They managed to scramble up on to the plinth.

Excitedly Elsa touched one of the coffins, its carvings more ornate than the rest. She ran her scholarly eye over it.

"Look at the scrollwork. This must be it."

They hardly dared to speak as they strained and pushed to get the lid of the coffin open. At last it slid off, bounced at their feet and disappeared into the water.

They stared into the open coffin.

The decomposed remains of a knight in armour looked back at them, hollow-eyed.

"This is it!" cried Indy. "Look at the engraving on the shield! It's the same as the Grail Tablet! The *shield* is the second 'marker'. The final clue, Elsa."

"I just wish your father were here to see it," she said, with emotion.

"Huh. He would never have made it past the rats. He's scared to death of 'em! We had one in the basement once. Guess who had to go down there and kill it? And I was only *six*!"

Carefully Indy brushed away the dust and corrosion on the Knight's shield. Then he took a piece of paper out of his pocket, handling it with utmost delicacy, and placed it over the top of the shield. It was his father's rubbing of the Grail Tablet, the tablet now in Donovan's apartment.

It matched up perfectly. The missing part of the inscription was now staring at him from the shield. The jigsaw was complete.

"Where did you get that?" asked Elsa sharply.

"Trade secret," said Indy. With a soft pencil he worked quickly to take a rubbing of the missing portion, then returned both to his waterproof pocket.

"I see." Elsa looked hurt. "I thought we were partners."

"Hold it!" hissed Indy. They both froze.

Something was badly wrong. Firelight was flickering and dancing on the walls of the burial chamber, getting brighter and brighter. A huge orange fireball was heading this way down the narrow passageway, back around the corner the way they'd just come. It was feeding on the oil slick, consuming all the oxygen.

But before the fireball came the rats: a huge tidal wave of them, fleeing in front of the fireball.

The rats washed right over their heads.

Then Indy saw the fireball. He braced himself against the stone plinth, kicking the open coffin into the water as he did so.

"Jump!" he shouted.

They plunged into the black water and into the bobbing upturned coffin. "Air pocket. Our only hope."

They had to share the air pocket with the grinning skull of the long-deceased knight until Elsa managed to unwedge the corpse. Weighed down by its suit of armour it sank out of sight.

No sooner had they got rid of the corpse than they were joined by rats, fleeing the fireball above.

Everything was on fire. Even the coffin was on fire now. It was getting hot in here! More rats were crowding him.

"Can you swim, Elsa?" rapped Indy.

"Austrian swim team, 1932 Summer Olympics," she rapped back.

They took deep lungfuls of the last bit of air left in the burning coffin, then dived.

They swam underwater, through a broken section of wall, then up a long tunnel. They swam on and on, then, almost at their last gasp, they saw it. A faint light. They had been swimming through a storm drain! There was daylight ahead!

The daylight came from a deep shaft that was driven into the storm drain from above. They got their upturned faces into the shaft in the nick of time and gulped in great lungfuls of air.

Then, once they'd recovered breath, they writhed and squirmed their way up the long shaft towards the daylight at the top.

They emerged into a beautiful sunlit square. People sipping drinks at open-air restaurants looked at the wet, smelly pair in amazement.

Indy took in some good deep gulps of air and looked at the picture postcard scene. "Ah, Venice!"

Then he whirled.

"Look out, Elsa!"

Three men in fezzes were heading towards them, their guns drawn. They were led by Kazim.

Indy grabbed Elsa's hand and they raced to a nearby jetty. They leapt into a motor boat and roared off.

The events that followed made the catacombs outing seem like a tea party.

Kazim and his men seemed intent on liquidating Indy and Elsa. They all played cat and mouse across the water, in and out of boats, dodging gun fire. At one time their speedboat was forced between two giant steamers and almost crushed to matchwood. Indy found a gap and squeezed through, with inches to spare.

Twice their boat was forced into the path of a powerful paddle steamer, its churning propellor ready to cut their vessel to ribbons.

And all the time Indy was mystified. Why were they trying to kill them? Was it to do with the Grail? Were these his father's enemies? They must be!

At last Indy got Kazim by the throat.

They were in a boat alone, drifting back into the path of that cruel propellor, about to be sliced into bacon.

"All right! Now talk!" snapped Indy. "Otherwise see that propellor . . .?"

"You foolish man. What are you doing, Dr. Jones?"

"Where's my father?"

"Let go of me, please," said Kazim. But he showed no fear.

Where's my father?

"If you don't let go, Dr. Jones, we'll both die."

"I don't care!" said Indy hysterically. This man unnerved him.

"Then we'll die," shrugged Kazim. "My soul is prepared — how is yours?"

Kazim's shirt ripped away in Indy's hand. Indy recoiled at what he saw there.

A cruciform sword was tattooed on the man's chest. The sight of it brought Indy to his senses. As Elsa brought another boat speeding alongside, Indy grabbed the man and they both jumped clear of the whirling blades with only moments to spare.

As they chugged away, Indy demanded:
"Who are you?"

"My name is Kazim. My forebears were princes of an Empire that stretched from Morocco to the Caspian Sea."

"And why are you trying to kill me?"

"And me?" added Elsa.

"The secret of the Grail has been safe for a thousand years. And for all that time the Brotherhood of the Cruciform Sword has

been prepared to do anything to keep it safe. Perhaps you would like to bring the boat in here. This jetty is convenient for my hotel.''

Silent and respectful, Indy obliged.

"Thank you," nodded Kazim. Stepping out of the boat, he added: "Ask yourself why you seek the Holy Grail — for the Lord's glory or for yours?"

"I didn't come for the Holy Grail. I came to find my father."

The man's expression softened.

"In that case, God be with you in your quest. Your father is being held in the Castle of Brunwald on the Austrian–German border."

Kazim gave a bow and walked away.

AT BRUNWALD CASTLE

Back in their apartment, Marcus and Indiana stared in excitement at the rubbing taken from the shield of the Grail Knight. Marcus was so excited that even the bump on his head stopped hurting.

"The missing part of the inscription. And it gives us the information we need. The name of the city. *Alexandretta*!"

"The Knights of the First Crusade laid siege to Alexandretta for over a year," recalled Indy. He was checking through an Atlas. "The entire city was destroyed . . . Here!" he stabbed his finger onto a map. "*Iskenderun*! That's it! The present city of Iskenderun is built on the ruins of Alexandretta."

Marcus peered over his shoulder at the map in joy.

"And look, Marcus — this is the desert and this is the mountain range. Just the way the Grail Tablet describes it. Somewhere in these mountains must be the Canyon of the Crescent Moon and the Temple of the Sun. But where?"

"Your father knows," said Marcus quietly. He opened the Grail Diary. Luckily Kazim had known nothing about its existence when he cracked him on the head. "Look, Indy. The centre pages."

"A sketch map!" exclaimed Indy. "A map with no names. The route to the Canyon of the Crescent Moon from an unknown town. *And we now know which town*."

"Henry will have pieced this map together from a hundred different sources over the last forty years," said Marcus gratefully.

Indy took the precious Grail Diary and tucked it in his pocket. Right. Now for action.

"Marcus, you go straight to Iskenderun. Contact Sallah. Have him meet you there. He'll look after you."

Sallah was an old friend; completely trustworthy.

"What about you?"

"I'm going after Dad," said Indy.

★★★   ★★★

Indy's bedroom had been ransacked. Elsa's suite along the corridor had been ransacked, too.

"What were they looking for, Indy?"

"This," he replied. He tossed the Grail Diary down in front of her.

"The Grail Diary! *You* had it?" she exclaimed. Then she looked hurt. "You didn't trust me."

"I do now," he said, touching her face gently.

"Look after me, Indy."

"You looked after yourself pretty well today — for an art historian."

"Do you know anything about art historians?"

"I know what I like."

They drove out of Italy the next day and on to Austria. The following day they reached Brunwald Castle, high up in the Austrian mountains, close to the German border. Storm clouds gathered around it. It looked a grim, forbidding place.

As they parked Elsa's Mercedes-Benz and got out, Indy adjusted his brown hat and took his bull whip from the car. He had the feeling he might need it.

A butler let them in. But he didn't believe they'd come to look at tapestries, as Indy claimed. So Indy knocked him out cold and put him in a cupboard.

They crept into the main hallway, then froze. There were Nazis walking around inside the castle. Nazis everywhere in their brown shirts, swastika armbands and jack-boots.

"I should have known," he whispered.

They found a hiding-place and kept watch.

"Now where do you suppose they're holding Dad?"

"The dungeon?" suggested Elsa.

"No — look!" hissed Indy.

A servant was coming down the main staircase carrying a cheap little tray with an empty tin bowl on it. A Nazi soldier escorted him. That had obviously been Dad's supper.

"He's upstairs somewhere. Come on."

They explored the upper floors, dodging roaming Nazis as they went.

Until at last . . .

"He's in that room there," whispered Indy, pointing to a massive door. There was new electrical wiring all round it. "The door's wired up. Electrified, I guess."

He found an adjacent room, went inside and flung open the window shutters. Outside the rain was coming down in sheets. He clambered out onto the wide slippery window ledge. There was a gap of several yards to the window ledge where he was sure his father was a prisoner.

"What are you going to do, Indy?" asked Elsa.

"Don't worry. This is kid's stuff. Wait here."

He snaked his bull whip through the air so that the end wrapped itself round and round a stone gargoyle that protruded from the castle walls. Then, with one quick glance at the sheer drop beneath, he gripped the handle of the whip tight and swung himself through the air to his father's window ledge.

The window was shuttered. He rattled the shutters fiercely but they wouldn't budge. Down below Nazis were patrolling with dogs, their flashlight beams stabbing up towards him. He had to act fast!

Gripping the handle of the whip he swung himself off the ledge again and into space, round in an arc.

CRASH!

Using his feet as a battering ram he splintered the shutters into matchwood and smashed through into the room. He landed on his knees.

Even as he started to rise to his feet . . . CRACCKKK!

He was hit on the head with a vase. Stunned, he dropped back down on his knees again. A man stepped out of the shadows.

"JUNIOR!"

"Er — yessir."

Still holding the smashed vase in his hand, Professor Henry Jones stared at his son in bewilderment.

"It's you, Junior!"

"*Would you stop calling me that?*"

"What are you *doing here*?" asked Indy's Dad in amazement.

"What do you think? I've come to get you!"

Full of emotion they both started talking at once. Indy told his father everything that had happened to date.

"Alexandretta," murmured Henry, over and over again. "Of course . . . on the pilgrim trail from the Eastern Empire. Part of ancient Antioch. Protected by Syria.

Desired by Turkey. *Junior* . . ." Indy winced. "Junior, you did it."

"No, Dad, you did. Forty years of research and scholarship."

He gazed round the huge room, looking for a way out.

"What do the Nazis want with you, Dad?"

"The Grail Diary."

No sooner were those words spoken than three Nazis kicked open the door. Two of them had machine guns. Their officer walked straight up to Indy.

"I'll take the Diary now. I know you have it in your pocket.

"You dolt!" laughed Henry. "Do you think my son would be stupid enough to bring the Diary all the way back to danger?" His voice trailed away as he saw the sheepish expression on his son's face. "Oh no! I should have mailed it to the Marx Brothers," he groaned. "*Junior*."

Indy's eyes blazed and his nostrils flared. He ripped a machine gun from the hands of the nearest soldier.

"I told you before, Dad," he cried as he pumped bullets into all three Nazis, "don't call me Junior!"

His father stared at the corpses in horror. "Look what you did. I can't believe what you did!"

"Out," said Indy, propelling his father from the room. "Let's pick up Elsa and go. She's waiting for us next door."

As they entered the room where he'd left Elsa, he went pale.

A brutish Nazi Colonel was pressing the muzzle of a Luger gun against her head.

"Put down the machine gun or the Fraulein dies," snapped Colonel Vogel.

"Don't listen, son!" pleaded his father. "She's a Nazi."

"*What*? What are you talking about, Dad?"

"Indy, please do as he says, drop the machine gun," begged Elsa.

"Trust *me*," gritted Henry.

"I'll kill her!" said the Colonel, pressing the Luger closer.

"He won't," growled Henry.

"Enough! She dies!"

The Colonel jabbed the muzzle hard behind Elsa's ear and she screamed. Indy's nerve gave. "Wait!" he yelled.

He dropped the machine gun to the floor and kicked it away. As he did so, Colonel Vogel prodded Elsa in the back with the Luger — propelling her straight into Indy's arms.

"I'm sorry, Indy." She embraced him tightly, then slipped her hand into his pocket and took out the Grail Diary. "I'm so terribly sorry. But your father was right. You should have listened to him."

And she handed the Diary to Colonel Vogel.

It gave Indy a terrible shock.

Under armed guard, he and Henry were taken into the castle's huge baronial hall with their hands tied behind their backs.

There was an even greater shock to come.

Elsa strode towards a figure concealed in a high-backed chair. A hand reached out and took the Grail Diary.

"How did you know she was a Nazi?" Indy was saying.

"I heard her talk in her sleep once. She

said, *Mein Führer.*"

"Pretty conclusive, Dad. So she ransacked her rooms *herself* and I fell for it."

"I didn't trust her," said his father accusingly, "Why did *you*?"

"*Because he didn't take my advice,*" said a voice from the highbacked chair.

The man rose to his feet and turned to face them. He flicked through the Grail Diary, with a benign smile.

"Didn't I warn you not to trust anybody, Dr. Jones?"

"Donovan!" gasped Indy. "Walter Donovan!"

"So it's you, Walter," said Henry, sourly. "I always knew you'd sell your mother for an Etruscan vase but I didn't know you'd sell your country and your soul to this bunch of madmen."

But as he examined the Diary, Donovan paled.

"The centre pages have been removed! The map! Come here, Dr. Schneider, what's the meaning of this? *Where's the map?*"

Elsa rushed over to Donovan.

"Of course!" she realized. "He sent Marcus Brody ahead to Syria — to Iskenderun. He'd have given Brody the map to take with him!"

"Oh, Junior, you didn't drag poor Marcus along, did you? He's not up to the challenge," whispered Henry.

"We'll find Brody," snapped Donovan.

"Not a chance," bluffed Indy. "He's got a head start — knows twelve languages — knows the terrain. Most likely found the Grail by now."

Henry looked pleased and impressed at this description of his best friend. In fact Marcus had once got lost in his own museum!

And, true to form, having met up with Sallah in Iskenderun, Marcus Brody had already let himself be captured by a group of Nazis.

At that very moment they were taking him away in a troop truck, leaving Sallah beaten up and senseless in the dusty Eastern street.

6

A BRUSH WITH HITLER

Father and son were marched into another room and tied up, back to back, in a huge baronial fireplace. Elsa and Donovan stood watching. But suddenly Colonel Vogel appeared.

"Dr. Schneider, urgent message from Berlin. You are to return immediately. The Führer wants your presence on the platform. A rally at the Institute of Aryan Culture."

"Thank you, Herr Colonel." Elsa clicked her heels. "I am deeply honoured." She turned to Walter Donovan. "I'll meet you at Iskenderun, Walter."

"We'll have the map by then," said Donovan confidently. He handed Elsa the Grail Diary. "This is no more than a worthless souvenir now. Give it to the Reich Museum in Berlin. They'll be pleased to see we're ahead of schedule."

To Indy's deep disgust, Elsa came over and tried to kiss him goodbye.

"Don't look at me like that — we both wanted the Grail. I would have done anything — you would have done the same."

"I'm sorry you think so," said Indy, jerking his head away.

Before she left in her Mercedes-Benz, Elsa requested Colonel Vogel not to kill them. He agreed, but only to humour her.

If Indy hadn't managed to burn through their bonds with his father's cigar lighter, accidentally setting fire to the room and the Nazi soldiers who were guarding them, they would certainly have been killed.

Instead, after a hair-raising chase, they escaped from Brunwald Castle. They then commandeered a passing motor-cycle with sidecar. And as they roared along, past a crossroads:

"Stop!" shouted Henry. "Why are we heading for Budapest?"

"Because that's the way to Iskenderun," shouted Indy, pulling up with a scream of brakes. "The other way's Berlin."

"That's where my Diary is," moaned his father.

"We don't need it now."

"You're wrong, son. When we locate the Grail there are some final devices of lethal cunning. Eight years ago I found the clues that would take us safely through. I found them in the Chronicles at St. Anselm. I wrote them in the Diary — but I can't remember them."

They ducked out of sight as two Nazi motor-cyclists went screaming past. Then Indy looked at his father in fury.

"The Gestapo and half of Hitler's storm-troopers are after us now — and you want to turn around and head for Berlin, right into the lion's den."

"Yes. The only thing that matters is the Holy Grail."

"The only thing that matters is Marcus!"

"No, son. And Marcus would agree with me."

"You scholars!" raged Indy. "Pride and plunder! *Jeez*- . . ."

His father struck him across the face. Not a hard blow, but the force of his anger rocked Indy to the foundations.

"That's for blasphemy. The quest for the cup is *not* archaeology, it's a race against evil. If the Grail is made captive to the cult of the Nazis, the armies of the darkness will march over the face of the earth. Do you understand me?"

They set off for Berlin.

Disguised in Nazi uniforms, Dr. Indiana Jones and his father the professor were pressed in a shop doorway. They were in Berlin; the main city square lay just ahead.

Crowds cheered, flags fluttered, banners swayed.

A 1930s Nazi rally was at its height.

Up on the podium, in front of the Institute of Aryan Culture, was Adolf Hitler. On one side of him stood a lumpish-looking woman with grey hair, the Minister of Art Acquisitions. On the other side of him stood the lovely Dr. Elsa Schneider.

The rally ended with thunderous applause and the crowds started to stream away. Elsa was the first person off the podium. As she strode towards her Mercedes-Benz Indy darted out of the shadows, his arms outstretched.

He swept her to his chest in an iron grip.

"Fraulein Doctor."

"Indy. You followed me. You love me. You came back for me?"

"Uh uh . . ." Indy squeezed her even tighter, his hands running all over her body, feeling feverishly for . . .

The Grail Diary! He whisked it out of her pocket and held it up.

"Not for you. For this — the book."

He pushed the disappointed Elsa away and ran.

"Come on Dad. Now let's get out of here."

They ran round a corner — straight into a crowd of boys who were standing on tiptoes and waving their autograph books.

A tight knot of men was approaching. The Führer, protected by his bodyguard, was strutting this way, signing autographs as he went.

Hitler reached Indy, then pulled up. His searching little evil eyes met Indy's. It was an electrifying moment — a moment of pure terror. What, wondered Hitler, was one of his crack storm-troopers doing here with a gang of schoolboys? He should be on crowd control.

Indy bared his teeth in what passed as a smile and proffered the Grail Diary, open at the inside cover.

Hitler visibly relaxed. Gratified, he autographed it and then swept on.

As Indy and Henry made their way back to their motor-bike combination, a very fat S.S. officer barred their path.

"What are you doing here? This is a restricted area! Get back to your post at once!"

Indy raised his arm in a Heil Hitler salute. Slowly his outstretched palm curled up into a fist.

CRUNCH.

Indy's fist smashed into the S.S. officer's jaw and knocked him out cold. He stole the man's overcoat, donned it, then off they zoomed on the motor-bike.

"Right. We've got the Diary back. Now we're gonna do things my way!"

"What does that mean?" asked Henry.

"We're getting out of Germany."

But as they lined up for a plane at Berlin Airport, Colonel Vogel suddenly appeared. Not five yards away from them he spoke to the Gestapo officers who were manning the boarding gates and showed them a photograph of Henry.

Indy and Henry quickly turned up the collars of their Nazi overcoats, pulled down their peaked caps — and ran.

Straight over to the VIP air terminal. A stewardess was ushering a line of prosperous-looking people out onto the tarmac beyond. To celebrate Hitler's birthday, a joy ride to Athens in a Zeppelin had been arranged. The massive airship was moored outside, just waiting to go. It was ten storeys high and a wondrous sight.

"Lucky break!" whispered Indy.

Father and son tagged on to the end of the line, smiled at the good-looking stewardess — and were ushered onto the tarmac to board the Zeppelin.

7

DEATH IN THE SKIES

Vogel and a Gestapo agent boarded the Zeppelin just two minutes before departure.

Indy knew how to deal with them.

Disguising himself as an official, he walked along the rows checking tickets.

When he reached Vogel, he lifted him up bodily and hurled him from a window of the airship, seconds before it rose gently into the sky.

"No ticket," he explained, to the horrified passengers.

The Gestapo agent, whom he found prowling the corridors of the airship, he clubbed on the head and locked in a cupboard.

Father and son then relaxed in the airship lounge.

"In a few hours we'll join up with Marcus and go after the Grail," said Indy. "Let's hope he's looking after your map, Dad. Right now we can sit back and enjoy the ride. Quite a guy, Count Zeppelin. Fought on the Federal side in the Civil War."

At a nearby table a famous German flying ace from the far more recent First World War was reliving his exploits with a model aeroplane. The other passengers enjoyed this diversion and kept plying him with drinks.

"He's getting very drunk," commented Indy.

But Henry was busy. He had the Grail Diary open, frowning in concentration.

"Here are the sketches of the three lethal devices that guard the Grail. The pendulum, the cobbles and the bridge. And here are the secret ways through, from the Chronicles of St. Anselm."

He read from his Diary, quietly:

"The challenges will number three. First, the breath of God, only the penitent man will pass. Second, the word of God, only in the footsteps of God will he proceed. Third, the path of God, only in the leap from the lion's head will he prove his worth."

"Meaning what?" asked Indy.

"I think we'll find that out when we get there," replied his father. "What's the matter *now*?"

Indy had jumped to his feet. The airship was turning round! Turning round and going back to Berlin!

The Gestapo agent had smashed his way out of the cupboard and alerted the pilot! Now he came into the airship lounge, waving his arms:

"Attention everyone! There are spies aboard the airship! Everyone loyal to the Führer and the Third Reich come immediately with me."

The passengers smiled, yawned and resumed their chatter and their cocktails. Only some crew members volunteered — and the First World War air ace, wobbling drunkenly. The Gestapo man quickly organized a search party.

"Come on, Dad, we'd better beat it," said Indy, pushing his father out through a hatch. They found themselves inside the Zeppelin's massive outer frame. The gas-bags that kept it airborne were suspended somewhere underneath.

"Walk along this catwalk, Dad. We've got to try and reach one of the biplanes."

There were two small biplanes suspended below the airship for emergencies, rather like lifeboats on board ship.

They climbed through an exit, out of the Zeppelin's great frame. A ladder suspended in space led down to the first biplane. There was nothing around them but sky and more sky. The ground was a thousand feet below.

Henry was safely on the ladder when a crew member reached out from the exit door and dragged Indy back inside. A fierce fist fight developed. Soon, both men were teetering dangerously in the doorway on the very brink of death. Then Henry crawled back up the ladder, grabbed the crew member by the seat of his trousers and threw him off. Into space.

"AAARGH!" cried the man as he plummeted.

"Look what you did," said Henry indignantly.

"*Me*?"

They both scrambled down the ladder now and into the open biplane. Indy sat in the cockpit, his father behind him.

"I didn't know you could fly a plane," said Henry with pleasure.

"Fly, yes," replied Indy. "Land, no."

The Gestapo agent appeared at the exit above them. He squinted down the barrel of his pistol, aiming for Indy's head.

"Nein!" shouted a crew member, jerking at the man's arm and pointing to the gas bags near Indy's head. "VVVRRMMMM!" he explained. Thanks to that arm jerk, the bullet missed.

Indy quickly released the plane, let it drop clear of the airship and opened throttle.

Meanwhile the drunken First World War ace had found the ladder into the second biplane and was slithering down it eagerly. "Come! Come!" he cried.

Obediently the Gestapo agent leapt out of the Zeppelin. It was a twelve-foot drop into the rear seat of the second biplane. His legs went straight through the fuselage, splintering it to matchwood. Thud!

"Achtung!" cried the air ace from the cockpit, hearing the passenger thump into place behind him.

Drunkenly he released the plane. Too drunk to remember to turn on the engine.

Eee . . owww . . owww . .

The plane spiralled silently, faster and faster towards the ground. The air ace was crouched eagerly over the joy stick.

The Gestapo agent's legs were still sticking through the bottom of the plane.

CRASH!

That was the end of them.

★★★   ★★★

As Indiana's plane hummed along through clear blue skies, he turned in the cockpit and gave Henry the thumbs-up sign.

Hours later, somewhere over Turkey, two Messerschmidt fighter planes screamed past them on either side.

"The machine gun!" yelled Indy. It was mounted to the back of the plane.

Fumblingly Henry got hold of it and found the trigger.

RATTA-TAT-A-TAT!

Ahead of them the Messerschmidts banked steeply and came back this way, their own guns firing. Henry swung the machine gun right round to take aim again.

"Whoops!" he muttered under his breath.

He'd knocked off the plane's fragile tail-piece.

Indy struggled with the controls as the plane started dropping fast. The ground was rushing up at them.

"They got us," his father fibbed.

"Hold on. We're going in!" cried Indy, struggling to make a controlled landing. He could see a good clear stretch of road below.

CRR . . CRR . . UNCH!

Indy managed to belly-land the plane but it skidded out of control. It came to rest on its side, right by a tavern.

They leapt out, just as a customer tottered from the tavern, making for a battered automobile.

Indy elbowed the Turk out of the way of his car and jumped in the driving seat himself. Henry tumbled into the rear seat.

Indy revved up the engine and they raced away.

"Hey, that's my car!" shouted the man, running down the road after them, waving his arms.

Then he saw two screaming Messerschmidts coming in low, guns blazing. He dived into the nearest field and rolled out of the way of the flying shrapnel.

Indy drove flat out. His father cowered in the back. The Messerschmidts were strafing them. Shrapnel whistled through the car roof and past their ears! But just ahead of them the road went into a mountain tunnel!

The car squeaked into the tunnel ahead of the leading Messerschmidt, just as it did a bomber dive at them. And so — BOOMMM!

The German fighter hit the mouth of the

tunnel at speed. Its wings sheared off. The fuselage went up in flames. As the fuel ignited it became a raging fireball.

A fireball that was pursuing them down the tunnel!

As they came out of the tunnel at the other end, the fireball passed straight over their heads and landed on the road in front of them. Indy couldn't stop.

"We'll have to charge straight through the flames, Dad!"

They made it. Henry mopped his brow. "They don't come any closer than that!"

"Yes they do, Dad," said Indy. The second Messerschmidt was right overhead. Something was dropping from its under-carriage — A bomb.

It exploded on the road ahead. Indy swung hard at the steering wheel to avoid it. The car skidded out of control, left the road and bounced down a grassy embankment. It came to rest embedded in deep, soft sand.

Indy helped his father out. They were on a southern Mediterranean beach. Beautiful sand. Lapping waves. A picturesque flock of gulls perched all around the beach.

And the Messerschmidt coming in low for the last time, its machine guns firing.

The startled seagulls rose into the sky in a great dark cloud of flapping wings — straight into the path of the fighter plane.

The birds were sucked into the whirling propellor, wrecking the engine. There was a splutter as the engine died. Then silence.

Then came a massive explosion as the crippled plane hit the sea.

For the gulls, tragedy. Death in the skies.

For Indiana and Henry Jones, triumph. Against all the odds, they'd survived.

"Now we've got to get to Iskenderun and find Marcus," grunted Indy.

"And the Holy Grail," added Henry firmly.

They were only a hundred miles from Iskenderun now.

A TERRIBLE BATTLE

As Indiana and Henry stepped off the train at Iskenderun next day, Sallah rushed up to them. Still bruised and battered from being beaten up, he had been keeping an anxious lookout for them.

"The enemy has got a head start! They set off across the desert this afternoon," he cried. "Quick, into the car. There is no time to lose."

"Where's Marcus?" they asked in dismay.

"They have him prisoner. They have the map! They are even now on their way to collect the Grail. A whole army of them!"

Walter Donovan and Elsa Schneider together with Colonel Vogel were leading the expedition. They had taken Marcus with them. And two Nazi troopcarriers.

Furthermore the ruler of the province, a powerful Sultan, had taken a fancy to the Nazi's staff car. It was the car he had always wanted, a Daimler-Benz 3.4 litre.

In return for this car, the Sultan had given their expedition across his territory his blessing. Even more helpful, he'd given them horses, camels, supply vehicles and an armed escort of his own best fighting men. He'd also lent them his pride and joy — a vintage First World War army tank. It was

one of the most powerful tanks ever built and still in good working order.

Formidable opposition.

Sallah put his foot down hard on the pedal and they went screaming through the streets of Iskenderun. Goats, bicycles, carpet sellers and pedestrians jumped clear as the horn blared. Henry cowered in the back of the car, shouting "Go faster, Sallah!"

As they left the town behind and took the desert road, Indy adjusted his brown fedora hat and fingered the handle of his bull whip.

It looked like a tough battle ahead.

Walter Donovan stood on top of the tank as the long procession wended its way through a steep desert valley. The sun was blisteringly hot. Marcus Brody was imprisoned inside the tank.

Donovan opened the hatch and offered him a drink.

"Wet your whistle, Marcus," he said to the helpless Englishman. He was feeling elated. "According to your map we're only three or four miles from the discovery of the greatest artefact in human history."

The imprisoned professor looked at him sourly.

"You're meddling with powers you cannot possibly contemplate."

As Donovan glanced back at the hill that they'd just descended, he stiffened. He'd caught the glint of sun on glass. He had already been informed by Colonel Vogel that Indiana Jones and his father had escaped from Brunwald Castle and then from Berlin. Could they be on the trail? Were they spying on them right now?

Was that the glint of sunlight on binoculars?

"Fire, Vogel!" he exclaimed, pointing.

The tank's main cannon was brought round and a shell despatched into the sky.

BRRMMMM!

High up on the hillside they saw a motor vehicle explode into the air and break into a thousand pieces.

"Bull's eye," said Colonel Vogel. Then he barked out: "Halt, everyone. We are going back to investigate."

Indy, Henry and Sallah kept their heads down behind some rocks.

"That was my brother-in-law's car," said Sallah sadly, looking across at the wrecked vehicle.

Indy lowered his binoculars.

"They're turning back. Coming to find us. Troop carriers, camels, horses, the lot. Even the tank. I'll think of something."

It was the horses he had his eye on mainly.

Elsa and Donovan examined the wrecked car. "No bodies," said Donovan in disappointment.

"They're here somewhere," said Elsa. "I just know it."

Suddenly from the caves all around came the rattle of gun fire. The Nazi soldiers and the Sultan's men ran around in circles, their guns spitting out bullets in reply.

"It's Kazim — it's the Brotherhood!" whispered Indy in amazement. "Defending the Grail to the death as he always said they would!"

Kazim led his men into pitched battle with the Nazis, lobbing hand grenades, firing furiously.

"This is our chance," whispered Indy urgently. "Stay hidden, Dad. Sallah and I will creep over there and grab some horses."

They had almost reached the horses when a Nazi soldier spotted them. He opened his mouth to raise the alarm but at the very same moment, Kazim had seen them, too.

Kazim shot the soldier before he could cry out.

Then he raced on towards Donovan with fanatical hatred in his eyes.

To save Indy and Sallah, Kazim had fired his last bullet. Now his gun was empty.

Donovan shot him at point-blank range.

"Who are you?" he snapped.

As Kazim sank to the ground he spat out his last words:

"A messenger from God. For the unrighteous the Cup of Life holds everlasting damnation." Then he died.

Hidden from sight, Indy and Sallah stealthily began to untie the horses.

Meanwhile, Henry had crept from his hiding-place to the tank. In the heat of the battle it had been left unguarded. And he'd seen his dear old pal Marcus, peering from the hatch!

Inside the tank the two old men embraced.

"Henry!"

"Marcus!"

"What are you doing here?"

"It's a rescue, old boy. What did you think?"

Except that the very next moment two Nazi soldiers dropped down into the tank, their Lugers drawn. They were followed by Vogel.

"Search him!" snapped the Colonel.

But there was no Grail Diary to be found on Henry.

"What is in the book, the miserable little book of yours?" asked Vogel, slapping him. "We have the map. The book is useless. And yet you went all the way back to Berlin to get it. Why? What does the Diary tell *you* that it doesn't tell *us*?"

"It tells me," replied Henry, "that goose-stepping morons like yourself should try reading books instead of burning them."

"Herr Colonel!" The tank commander appeared. "They've got some horses. They're escaping!"

"Exterminate them!" rapped Vogel, climbing up to have a look. "Give chase! They must die!"

Indy rode with fiendish skill as the tank lumbered along behind him. Huge shells exploded, first to his right, then to his left. Indy rode back and forth, round and round, until the tank driver became totally confused. Indy then led the tank on into a head-on collision with one of their own Nazi staff cars.

The car wedged between the giant treads of the tank, immobilizing it and blocking the view from the main gun turret. Indy then reined in his horse, scooped up some rocks and jammed them down the barrel of the tank's smaller side gun.

He then rode round, deliberately revealing himself to the side gunner. The gunner fired. But because the barrel was blocked with rocks the shell backfired in his face and blew him up.

The inside of the tank was filled with smoke. Choking for air, Vogel opened the hatch and came up for air, together with Henry and Marcus.

"Revenge!" shouted Vogel to the main gunner, who couldn't see a thing because of the car wedged on the tank treads. "Fire!"

The six pounder blew the car and the men inside it to smithereens.

Indy raced up a steep track until he was riding parallel to the lumbering tank and immediately above it. He leapt from the saddle and dropped on to the top of the tank.

He was face to face with Vogel. They stared at one another in hatred.

Then the troop carrier drew alongside and ten Nazi soldiers swarmed on board and fell on Indy. Indy grabbed a Luger and shot three of them, leaving only seven to go.

As Indy slugged away, Henry's head popped out of the hatch. "That's my boy! Go get 'em, Junior!"

"*Never call me Junior!*" raged Indy, kicking two more Nazis over the side into the tank's treads. Then he knocked out four more and kicked Vogel.

But Vogel came back at him and encircled him with a long thick chain. Writhing, Indy twisted until Vogel was caught in the chain with him.

Down below Henry saw the second troop carrier drawing alongside the tank with reinforcements. He squeezed the trigger of the cannon and blew the whole lot up.

But the blast blew Indy and Vogel, now wrapped together in the chain, onto their backs. Meanwhile Henry's guard below was

about to shoot him when Marcus jumped him from the back.

The bullet ricocheted seven times and ended up in the forehead of the tank driver.

The driver slumped over the controls. The tank started to trundle helplessly towards a ravine.

Henry and Marcus opened the hatch and climbed out on top of the tank. They watched in horror as Indy and Vogel struggled in the chains together, about to go over the side into the tank's treads at any moment.

Sallah came riding up and yelled to the old men to jump clear. Marcus jumped into the saddle behind Sallah.

But nobly Henry stayed on board, trying to help Indy by grabbing Vogel's feet.

Vogel simply kicked Henry over the side — onto the tank treads.

With lightning speed, Indy managed to get an arm free and flick his bull whip.

It wrapped itself tightly round his father's left ankle. He passed the handle up to Sallah who was riding alongside the runaway tank. Sallah slowed his horse to a standstill and gripped the handle of the bull whip tight.

Henry was thus tugged off the tank treads by the left ankle with only moments to spare. Now he was safe.

Meanwhile Indy and Vogel had rolled off the back of the tank just yards from the ravine, still locked together in combat and chains. And now the chain's trailing end got hooked up on the back of the tank!

They were being dragged along the ground together towards the ravine! Indy writhed and struggled, but the chain wouldn't budge. It was girdling his hips tightly. The only hope was to get his trousers down . . .

Vogel was screaming with terror as the tank pitched over the ravine. Henry, Marcus and Sallah looked down at the flaming wreckage of the tank, lying at the bottom of the ravine. They buried their faces in their hands.

"I can't believe he's dead," said Henry.
"I'm not, Dad."

Dazed and dishevelled, Indy stumbled out from behind some cacti, holding up his trousers with one hand. He had ripped them down and pulled clear of the chains on the very brink of the ravine!

"Now *that* was close," said Indy.

Henry gazed at his son. He was overcome with emotion. He placed his arms round him. "I thought I'd lost you, Henry Jones Junior."

Indy's head started to clear. His father had never hugged him before. It was great to have his approval. It was great to think they could be friends. As the others watched, moved by the reconciliation between father and son, Indy hugged him back. But he said: "You know I never liked that name. I'm Indiana, okay?"

It had been a terrible battle.

★★★   ★★★★

The four stood and surveyed the wreckage of the battlefield. Donovan and Elsa still had the map and were now racing on ahead towards the Holy Grail, escorted by the Sultan's men and the few surviving Nazi soldiers. Some horses and camels had been left behind. Indy, Henry, Marcus and Sallah mounted the freshest-looking animals.

Now for the last Crusade!

DEVICES OF LETHAL CUNNING

Later, riding through a mountain pass, they heard a distant explosion. It echoed and re-echoed round them.

"What was that?" asked Marcus.

"They've blown up a chunk of mountain-side," said Henry grimly. "Now they can enter the secret canyon. The Canyon of the Crescent Moon that leads directly to the Temple of the Sun — and the Grail."

"Nice of them to open it for us," said Indy in his soft, laconic voice. He adjusted his brown fedora under the scorching sun. It wouldn't be long now.

Soon they were riding along the canyon in the steps of the enemy. The sun scorched down hotter and hotter on the barren red rocks. Gradually the passageway between the canyon walls became narrower. They had to ride in single file. It was an eerie place.

"Antioch," mused Henry to himself. "Ancient Antioch."

The old man trembled at the thought that they were now approaching the Holy Grail: the culmination of his life's work.

"We're like the four heroes of the Grail legend," he exclaimed suddenly, as the four of them plodded wearily along. His voice echoed round the steep walls on either side. "You, Sallah, are Bors, the ordinary man. Marcus, you are Perceval, the holy innocent. You, Junior, are Galahad, the valiant knight."

"And you, Dad?"

"Galahad's father, Lancelot," replied Henry. "The old crusader. But remember, it was Galahad who succeeded where his father failed."

"I don't even know what the Grail looks like," shrugged Indy.

"Nobody does. The one who is worthy will."

Suddenly the canyon opened out. There in front of them was a most breathtaking sight: the entrance to a huge Grecian temple, its massive pillars reaching up into the clouds.

The Temple of the Sun!

Awestruck, they tethered the animals. They advanced silently up the marble steps, over the threshold and into the very temple itself. It was open to the skies — and a hundred times greater than the greatest cathedrals of the world. Quickly, they ducked and hid.

Something horrible was happening in the centre of the dark temple.

"Keep going, keep going," Walter Donovan was shouting.

"No, it's impossible," Elsa was protesting.

For one of the Sultan's men, his eyes wide with terror, was walking up a flight of steps. The steps led up to the mouth of a dark passageway. It was necessary to go through that to reach the Holy Grail. No wonder the man was terrified.

At the top of the flight of steps lay another of the Sultan's men. Beheaded. What had decapitated him?

"Keep going," insisted Donovan as the second soldier reached the top step, staring at his friend's head in horror. He whirled his sword about his own head to protect himself, trembling with fear. But . . .

WHOOSH!

Indy tensed as he heard that sudden rush of air. Then the second man's head flew off as his friend's had done. There was blood and gore everywhere. How was it happening? What mysterious force was guarding the entrance of the tunnel?

"No, No!" screamed another of the Sultan's men. Two Nazis had grabbed him and were propelling him towards the steps.

Marcus tried to stifle a cry of disgust — too late.

Suddenly they were surrounded. Dropped on from above.

Nazi guards relieved them of their pistols, rounded them up and made them put their hands up. Then, with the menacing Nazi rifles behind, they were forced to walk towards Donovan.

He looked at the group in unconcealed delight.

"Ah, the Jones boys . . . and not a moment too soon!"

Elsa rushed up to Indy.

"I never expected to see you again!"

"I'm like a bad penny. I always turn up."

"Move out of the way, Elsa," snapped Donovan. "We have a job for Dr. Jones. He's going to recover the Grail for us."

Indy glanced up the steps at the decapitated soldiers. And shuddered.

"Impossible?" asked Donovan. "What do you say, Dr. Jones? Ready to go down in history?"

"As what?" asked Indy. "A Nazi stooge, like you?"

"The Nazis?" said Donovan scornfully. "They merely want to write themselves into the Grail legend and take on the world. They're welcome. I want the Grail itself. The cup that gives everlasting life. Hitler can have the world but he can't take it with him."

He stepped forward and prodded Indy with his pistol. The uncomprehending Nazis who were guarding the four had no idea that their Führer was being insulted.

"I'm going to be drinking to my own health when Hitler has gone the way of the dodo," said Donovan. "The Grail is mine and you're going to get it for me."

"Shooting me won't get you anywhere," said Indy softly.

"You're absolutely right," smiled Donovan, at the same time taking a few steps backwards.

He turned and aimed his pistol straight at Henry.

"No!" cried Elsa, but he pushed her back.

Calmly, deliberately, he shot Indy's father in the stomach. Henry clutched his wound, turned in horror towards Indy, who ran and caught him in his arms as he fell.

"Dad, Dad," choked Indy.

He laid him gently on the ground. Sallah cradled his head while Marcus knelt beside his best friend, tears in his eyes. Grabbing a clean handkerchief from Sallah, Indy stuffed it against the gaping wound in his father's stomach, trying to staunch the flow of blood.

Then he straightened up and whirled on Donovan, his eyes blazing with hatred. "Why don't you kill *me*?"

"You can't save him when you're dead," said Donovan coolly. "The healing power of the Grail is the only thing that can save your father now. It's time to ask yourself what to believe."

"Indy, he's badly hurt," begged Sallah.

"Get the Grail, son. It's the only chance he's got," said Marcus.

Emotions raged inside Indy, while Donovan eyed him with a smirk. "Okay," Indy said at last. "You win."

He glanced up the steps at the decapitated soldiers.

Three devices of lethal cunning guard the Grail the old Chronicles had explained. The first one seemed to take your head off. How did you get through there? How did you get into that tunnel?

He took the Grail Diary out of his pouch and opened it. "Remember . . . the breath of God," gasped Henry, lying helpless at his feet. "That rush of air . . . you heard it? *Only the penitent man will pass.*"

Of course!

Covered by rifles, watched by Donovan, Indy slowly walked up the steps towards the mouth of the tunnel. He was reading from the Grail Diary as he went: desperately trying to puzzle it out.

"Only the penitent man will pass . . . *Only the penitent man will pass . . .*"

Each footstep brought Indy closer to the point of beheading. He stared down at the headless corpses, just inches in front of him. Then he looked upwards. Got it! he thought in excitement. The penitent man is humble. He *kneels* before God. Come on Indy, *kneel.*

WHOOSH! came the rush of air above him, just as he fell to his knees.

A triple pendulum whizzed around his head, its edges as sharp as razor blades, missing him by a hairsbreadth. Phew!

He crawled through the point of danger, found the mechanism that worked the fiendish device and jammed it. "I'm through!" he shouted.

Donovan and Elsa exhanged pleased nods and began to follow. "He's through," they said.

Indy entered the dark passageway and moved cautiously along, reading from the Grail Diary again. Now for the next test!

"*Proceed in the footsteps of the word. In the name of God.*"

He had reached a mass of cobblestones, laid out in front of him. Each was inscribed with a letter of the alphabet.

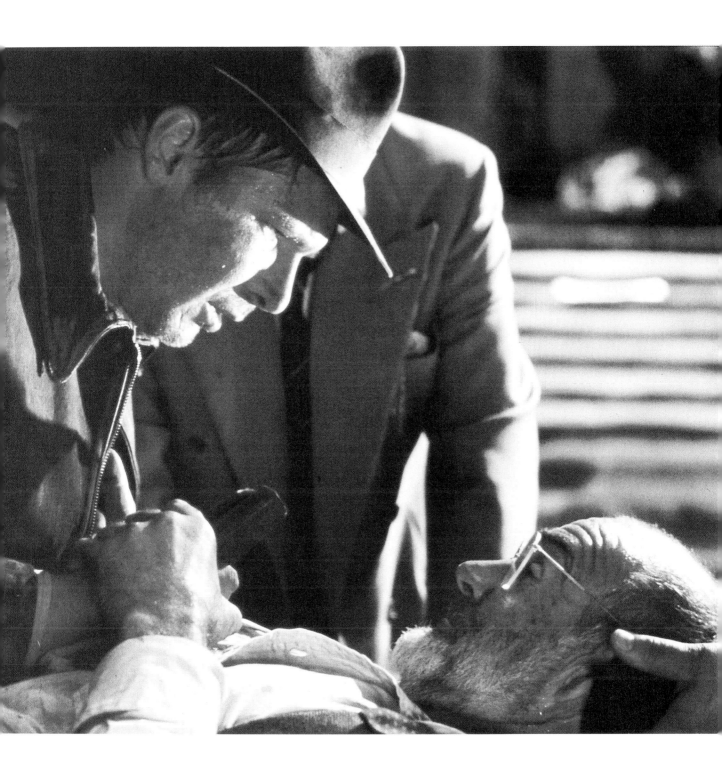

"*In the name of God*," puzzled Indy. What did it mean? Come *on*, he told himself. He *must* reach the Grail. His father lay dying out there. The name of — ? The name — of course! Got it! J—E—H—O—V—A. That was the name of God. He had only to step on each letter in turn, in the correct sequence . . .

Gingerly he stepped onto a cobblestone marked J.

Then he recoiled in horror. His foot had sunk into a hole and a giant, hairy black spider came clutching out at his leg. Indy jumped backwards to get free of it.

What have I done wrong? he puzzled anxiously. Then he remembered. *No J.* How stupid of me. No J in the Latin alphabet. They always used an *I* instead.

He leapt from cobble to cobble, shouting the letters out loud as he went, in something like triumph.

"I — E — H — O — V — A!"

A little way back along the passageway, those behind him heard and took note. Indy was making it all so easy for them!

But as he came out at the far end of the tunnel, Indy recoiled in horror. He was on the edge of an abyss. He was standing on top of something carved in the mountain rock. A lion's head.

"*The path of God,*" read Indy from the Grail Diary. "*Only in the leap from the lion's head will he prove his worth.*"

Indy stared across the yawning abyss in dismay.

"Impossible! Nobody can jump this!"

Meanwhile his father's pulse was getting weaker. His strength was ebbing away. As Sallah cradled his head Henry whispered urgently to the empty air. "You must believe, boy. You have to believe."

Marcus ran up to the dark entrance where the beheaded men lay. He called through the passageway in desperation.

"Indy — Indy. Quick, it's your father."

Standing on the lion's head, staring at that abyss, those words echoed in Indy's ears. But he knew that only the Grail could save his father now. He must go on! He must believe.

He pressed his back against the rock behind him, bent his knees, flexed his calf muscles, closed his eyes, and leapt!

He expected to plunge to the rocks a hundred feet below. Instead, he felt no more than a jarring to the back, a slight wobble around the knees. He opened his eyes . . .

And laughed.

He was only a few feet down, just below his line of vision when atop the lion. He was on solid ground, brilliantly camouflaged to look like a sheer drop. He was on a secret path. Scattering red dirt as he went in order to mark the path for his return journey, he crossed. He glanced back. The path was clearly visible now.

He came to an opening in the rock face and crawled through a narrow passageway. When he emerged he was inside a small secret temple.

He was awestruck. On a long stone slab was an array of chalices that gleamed in the flickering candlelight. Perhaps a hundred or more. Many sizes, many shapes, some gold, some silver, some studded with jewels.

Suddenly he realised that a man was kneeling at an altar.

The man rose to his feet and turned. The candlelight flickered on him and Indy saw he was very old. On his tunic chest was the emblem of the cross.

He moved to attack Indy with his sword, then stumbled. Indy rushed up to him and helped him to his feet. Only then did the old man relax.

"I knew you would come. You see, my strength has left me."

It was the Grail Knight.

THE LAST TRUMP

"You are strangely dressed, for a knight," said the old man, looking at Indy's brown hat and the bull whip in his belt, in puzzlement.

"Well, I'm not exactly a knight. What do you mean?"

"I was chosen to find and guard the Grail because I was the bravest and most worthy," explained the Knight. "The honour was mine until another came to challenge me in combat."

He passed his sword to Indy, ceremoniously. "I pass this to you who vanquished me."

"Hey, look, let me explain . . ." began Indy.

Suddenly Donovan burst into the temple, pistol at the ready. Elsa Schneider was just behind him. He raced over to the great stone slab that held all the chalices, at the same time waving his gun in their direction.

"Okay. Which one is it?"

"You must choose," said the Knight calmly. "But choose wisely, for just as the true Grail will bring you life, the false Grail will take it from you."

"Look — this one, Walter, it must be this one!" exclaimed Elsa, with a sly little smile.

She had picked up the most magnificent of all the cups, its rubies and diamonds dancing and gleaming in the candlelight. She handed it to him, egging him on. He snatched it eagerly.

"Oh, yes." He held it up to the light. "It's more beautiful than I had ever imagined!"

Unable to control his impatience, he ran over to a fount of magic water and quickly scooped some into the cup. Then he raised the cup to his lips, closed his eyes, smiled in ecstasy and drank.

AARRRGH!

He started shaking all over from head to foot. His face began to distort with age, his hands to wither. As he staggered over to Elsa crying, "What . . . is . . . happening . . . to . . . me?" her sly smile turned to a scream of terror.

Skin was flying off, he was turning into a skeleton before their eyes. Indy rushed across and pushed Elsa away. Then, as the ancient skeleton blackened with age and crumbled to the ground in a cloud of dust, he kicked it away.

Elsa clung to Indy, sobbing with fright. He calmed her.

"You chose poorly," said the Knight.

Indy's eyes darted urgently along the rows of chalices. His father lay dying! There was no time to lose! Which one was the Grail Cup?

His eyes came to rest on a cup very different from the rest. It was of a dull hue, stark in its simplicity. He reached out and took it. Elsa glanced at him, holding her breath. Had he chosen correctly?

"Only one way to find out," said Indy, reading her mind.

He darted across, scooped in some of the water — and drank.

For a few dreadful seconds he closed his eyes, waiting and wondering. When he opened them the Knight was smiling at him.

"You have chosen wisely."

Henry was at his last gasp when Indy placed the cup to his lips and forced a few drops of water down his throat. "Drink, Dad!"

Henry's eyes remained closed; Marcus and Sallah watched, hardly daring to breathe.

Then Indy gently poured some of the precious water over his father's wound, before forcing the last few drops past his lips again.

Henry's eyes fluttered open. He gazed at his son and Indy gazed back. His strength was returning. He took the cup from Indy's hand and passed it slowly back and forth over his body.

Then, all pallor leaving him, he raised himself to a sitting position, still holding the cup.

The sight unnerved the Sultan's soldiers, who dropped their rifles and fled. The Nazi guards started to give chase but Sallah grabbed one of the fallen rifles and fired a shot in the air. "*Put down your weapons!*" The Nazis stopped in their tracks, dropped their guns and raised their hands in surrender. Sallah rounded them up and kept them under guard.

Dr. Elsa Schneider was watching everything closely.

Indy, still on one knee beside his father, suddenly saw a most wonderful light appear in Henry's eyes. Henry was gazing up at something in awe.

The Grail Knight had appeared at Indy's shoulder.

"I know you." Henry trembled with joy. "Yes, I know you."

"Were we comrades in arms?" asked the gentle knight.

"No, from the books," whispered Henry.

He placed the Grail Cup on the ground while Indy helped him to his feet. Now he could look at the Knight properly.

"But why are you so old?" asked Henry.

"Many times my spirit faltered and I would not drink from the cup — so I aged a year for every day I did not drink. But now at last I am released to death with honour, for this brave knight-errant has come to take my place."

"Dad," Indy butted in, looking very embarrassed, "there's a misunderstanding here."

"He's no knight-errant," explained Henry quickly. "Merely my errant son who has led an impure life . . . totally unworthy."

"Unworthy!" stressed Indy, nodding.

Sweetly and anxiously the old Knight then peered at the other three men in turn — Henry, Marcus, Sallah.

"Which of you is it to be then, brothers?"

They all shook their heads, sad to disappoint him.

"Then why have you come?"

"*For this*!" cried Elsa triumphantly, diving forward and snatching the Grail Cup from behind their backs. She raced towards the temple's exit, cup held aloft, gloating. "We've won!" she cried. "We've got it. The world's most priceless art treasure. Come on, you four, what are you waiting for?"

"No," murmured the Knight. "The Grail can never leave this place. Remaining here is the price of immortality."

"*Listen to him*!" shouted Henry urgently.

"You must not cross the seal," stated the Knight.

"*Elsa! Elsa, don't move!*" yelled Indy in grim warning.

"It's ours, Indy. Yours and mine!"

As she crossed the metal seal that marked the temple's threshold, the seal turned into a massive crack. Elsa was pitched to the ground. The Grail Cup rolled from her hand and where it came to rest another crack formed. Now the earth began to move and heave around. The first crack grew wider into an abyss, leaving Elsa clinging to the edge by her fingertips, crying with fear!

Like the last trump, a huge earth tremor shook the temple. Its columns started to buckle. Rubble showered down, more cracks opened. Indy heard the screams of the Sultan's men and the Nazi soldiers as they pitched into a chasm.

He crawled on his stomach over the heaving earth. He had to get Elsa! At the very edge of the abyss he managed to get hold of her hands and strained to hold her weight. "Junior! Junior!" cried Henry. "Let her be. Save yourself!" Panic registered in Sallah's eyes. "Indy. She is worthless."

But he was holding on to Elsa . . . holding on. Until she saw the Grail Cup, lying on the ledge just out of reach. She snatched one of her hands free of Indy's and started to reach out. Straining . . . straining . . . to get the Grail.

"Stop it, Elsa! leave it! I can't hold you like this, I'm losing you."

"I can reach it, Indy." Those were her last words.

She pitched screaming into the abyss to her death.

"Elsa!" She very nearly took him with her. Now he, too, dangled into the abyss, hanging on only by his fingertips.

His father got to him and grabbed both his hands, perspiring with the strain of holding his son's weight. And just as Elsa had done, Indy stared longingly at the Grail Cup suddenly overwhelmed by temptation. He tried to reach out a hand . . .

"INDIANA!" Henry had never used the name before.

The shock jerked Indy back to his senses. He allowed himself to be dragged, inch by inch, back to safety.

"Come on!" shouted Marcus urgently. He and Sallah had escaped from the temple and were waiting at the foot of the marble steps with the horses.

Nearing the exit, Indy looked around for his father.

Henry stood rooted to the spot, gazing back towards the centre of the temple. The Grail Knight stood there, a shimmering figure amidst the rubble. Rocks showered down about his head and jets of steam hissed up from the cracked earth at his feet.

Yet a mysterious sweet smile played round the old Knight's lips. He looked so peaceful, raising his right arm to them in farewell.

"Goodbye, gentle Knight," whispered Henry, as the shimmering figure slowly melted from his vision. "You kept faith with the Grail to the very end."

"Come on, Dad," said Indy.

He took his father's arm and hurried them both out of the temple, dodging showers of stones and dust on the way. At the bottom of the marble steps, they scrambled onto their waiting horses.

"After you, Junior!" shouted Henry, with sudden exuberance.

Indy touched the brim of his fedora hat and smiled.

"Yes *sir*."

He cracked his bull whip and led the gallop back along the canyon, still smiling.

It felt good to be alive.